Where I Mommy?

Where Is Mommy?

PAT CUMMINGS

I Like to Read®

HOLIDAY HOUSE • NEW YORK

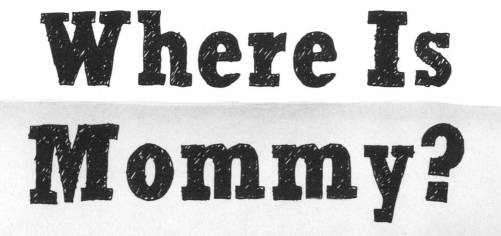

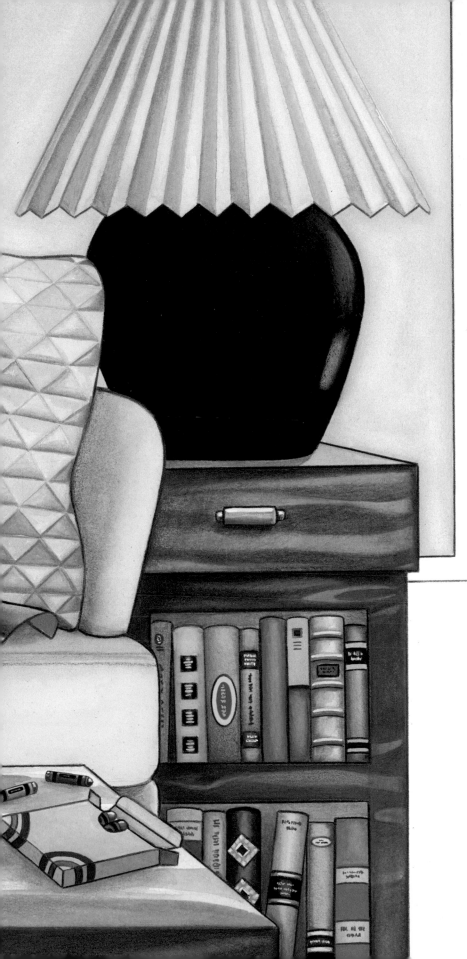

No, Max!

Where is
Mommy?

Here are her slippers.

Here are her glasses.

She must be
in her room.

She isn't under
the bed.

She isn't in
the closet.

But here is her scarf.

Mommy is missing!
We have to find her, Max.

Did you make this mess?

I have an idea!

I will make a picture of her.

What is that, Max?

Mommy tore this out.

Hey! Her hat is gone.
But her work gloves
are here.

Look, Max. There is fresh dirt on these gloves. I know where Mommy has been.

In the garden.
Mommy!

FOR EVA

I LIKE TO READ is a registered trademark of Holiday House Publishing, Inc.
Copyright © 2019 by Pat Cummings
All Rights Reserved
HOLIDAY HOUSE is registered in the U.S. Patent and Trademark Office.
Printed and bound in March 2019 at Tien Wah Press, Johor Bahru, Johor, Malaysia.
The artwork was created with watercolors, gouache, pencils, pastels,
and digital tools.
www.holidayhouse.com
First Edition
1 3 5 7 9 10 8 6 4 2

Library of Congress Cataloging-in-Publication Data
Names: Cummings, Pat, author, illustrator.
Title: Where is Mommy? / Pat Cummings.
Description: First edition. | New York : Holiday House, [2019]
Series: I like to read | Summary: "Fresh dirt, a kale recipe, and other clues lead
a girl to Mommy—in the garden!"—Provided by publisher.
Identifiers: LCCN 2018034828
ISBN 9780823439355 (hardcover)
ISBN 9780823439362 (pbk.)
Subjects: | CYAC: Mother and child—Fiction.
Mystery and detective stories.
Classification: LCC PZ7.C9148 Mom 2019
DDC [E]—dc23 LC
record available at https://lccn.loc.gov/2018034828